CONTENTS

KT-553-042

Raintree is an imprint of Capstone Global Library Limited, a
company incorporated in England and Wales having its
registered office at 264 Banbury Road, Oxford, OX2 7DY –
Registered company number: 6695582

www.raintree.co.uk
myorders@raintree.co.uk

Edited by Christopher Harbo
Designed by Brann Garvey
Originated by Capstone Global Library Ltd
Printed and bound in India

ISBN 978 1 4747 6404 9
22 21 20 19
10 9 8 7 6 5 4 3 2 1

British Library Cataloguing in Publication Data
A full catalogue record for this book is available from the British Library.

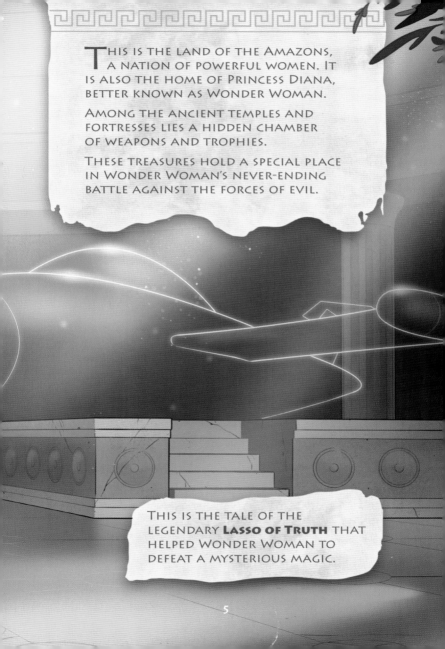

THIS IS THE LAND OF THE AMAZONS, A NATION OF POWERFUL WOMEN. IT IS ALSO THE HOME OF PRINCESS DIANA, BETTER KNOWN AS WONDER WOMAN.

AMONG THE ANCIENT TEMPLES AND FORTRESSES LIES A HIDDEN CHAMBER OF WEAPONS AND TROPHIES.

THESE TREASURES HOLD A SPECIAL PLACE IN WONDER WOMAN'S NEVER-ENDING BATTLE AGAINST THE FORCES OF EVIL.

THIS IS THE TALE OF THE LEGENDARY **LASSO OF TRUTH** THAT HELPED WONDER WOMAN TO DEFEAT A MYSTERIOUS MAGIC.

CHAPTER 1

A SCREAM AT SEA

The sun has set and the sailors on the SS *Orion* are afraid.

The ship left a port in Greece several weeks ago. It has just passed through the Panama Canal and is bound for Gateway City.

Every night for the last week, something strange has happened on the ship.

A sailor has disappeared.

The remaining sailors take turns keeping watch. A sailor called Davis is on patrol.

"Everything OK on deck, Davis?" asks a fellow sailor.

"Nice and quiet," says Davis.

AAAEEEEEEEHHH!

A scream rips through the night.

"That's coming from below!" says Davis.

He and the other sailor run towards the
sound. They rush down several flights of stairs.
Other sailors join them.

The ship's captain hurries down the stairs.
He pushes his way to the front of the crowd.

"The sound is coming from Jackson's
quarters," the captain says.

The men stand in front of the door to
Jackson's room. No one wants to open it.

"Stand aside," says the captain. He grabs the handle and turns it. The door swings open on heavy steel hinges.

"Jackson!" shouts the captain.

The room is empty.

CHAPTER 2

Wonder Woman is flying off the coast of Gateway City. She patrols the shipping lanes in her Invisible Jet.

Her jet flies over the SS *Orion*. An alarm lights up on the control board.

"S.O.S.," Wonder Woman says to herself. "That ship needs my help!"

Wonder Woman guides her jet down to the ship and lands on the deck.

"Wonder Woman!" cries the captain. "Thanks for answering our call for help."

The captain tells her about the strange string of disappearances.

Wonder Woman nods grimly. She looks up at the moon in the night sky.

"The sun won't come up for hours," she says. "I'll stay all night and patrol your ship."

Wonder Woman strides through the darkness. She patrols the silent decks.

She scans every shadow and checks every corner of the SS *Orion*.

AIIIEEEEEEEEEE!

Screams break the silence.

Wonder Woman runs towards the sound of the screams. She turns a corner and then stops.

Giant snakes are attacking two sailors.

CHAPTER 3

THE SORCERESS

The snakes twist their long purple bodies around the sailors.

Wonder Woman grabs her golden Lasso of Truth. She hurls the loop of the magic rope at the nearest snake.

The lasso passes through the creature's body as if it were made of smoke.

"Merciful Minerva!" cries Wonder Woman. She gathers the lasso to throw it at the slithering monsters again.

Suddenly, the men and the snakes disappear.

HAHAHAHAHAHA!

Wonder Woman recognizes that evil laughter. "Circe!" she shouts.

The sorceress appears before her in the cold moonlight.

"You can't defeat my illusions, Wonder Woman," says Circe. "My magic is more powerful than ever. When this ship reaches Gateway City, no one will stop me!"

Wonder Woman twirls her lasso again. But Circe melts into the air as she throws it.

What did Circe mean? thinks Wonder Woman.
Why will she be more powerful?

Wonder Woman quickly finds the captain.

"What cargo do you have on this ship?"
Wonder Woman asks.

"Mostly food and clothing," says the captain.
"Oh, and a special crate bound for the Gateway
City Museum."

"What's in the crate?" asks Wonder Woman.

The captain rubs his chin. "I'm not really sure. We picked it up in Greece."

Greece! thinks Wonder Woman. *Circe comes from ancient Greece.*

"Quickly," she says. "Take me to that crate!"

CHAPTER 4

THE MIRROR OF CIRCE

In a dark room far below deck sits the box from Greece.

The cabin door opens. Wonder Woman and the captain step inside.

"There it is." The captain points to the wooden box.

Wonder Woman opens the crate.

MMMMMMMMMMMM!

A humming sound comes from a glowing
mirror inside the crate.

Wonder Woman stares at the brightly gleaming object.

"The Mirror of Circe!" exclaims Wonder Woman. "It's been lost for a thousand years."

"And I'm not losing it again!" says a voice.

A flash of golden light fills the room. It blinds Wonder Woman.

When Wonder Woman opens her eyes, the captain has disappeared.

Now twelve Circes surround Wonder Woman.
Each one holds a mirror.

"My mirror can reflect many images of me,"
say all of the Circes. "With each image, my
power grows stronger."

"What have you done with the captain and his men?" demands Wonder Woman.

All of the Circes laugh.

"They're locked in a cargo hold," the Circes say together. "My snakes distracted them from my precious treasure."

All of the Circes face their mirrors towards Wonder Woman.

"And now you will join them!" scream the twelve sorceresses.

The mirrors begin to change shape.

In seconds, each Circe holds a purple chain in her hands. All of the chains twist and squirm like snakes.

The twelve chains shoot towards Wonder Woman. They quickly wrap around her, locking her in place.

CHAPTER 5

SHATTERING THE SPELL

The twelve Circes pull their chains tight.

How will I break free? thinks Wonder Woman. *And how will I know which Circe is real?*

As she struggles, Wonder Woman's hand brushes the rope on her belt.

"My magic lasso!" she shouts. Wonder
Woman tugs at the golden rope.

As soon as Wonder Woman grips her lasso,
the chains melt away.

"Your illusions can't overpower my Lasso of Truth," says Wonder Woman.

"The legendary lasso!" the Circes scream.

Wonder Woman twirls the shining lasso above her head. She flings the lasso towards all of the Circes.

The end of the golden rope touches each one.
The fake Circes shatter like broken mirrors.

Finally only one sorceress is left.

Circe tries to run, but Wonder Woman
catches her with the lasso.

"And now, Circe, show me where you're holding the men," says Wonder Woman.

The Lasso of Truth forces Circe to behave. She hands the mirror to Wonder Woman.

"This way, Wonder Woman," says the defeated sorceress.

Later that morning, the SS *Orion* docks in Gateway City. Its crew is safe.

The sailors surround Wonder Woman and thank her.

"What will happen to the sorceress?" asks the captain.

"She's going to prison," Wonder Woman says, handing him the Mirror of Circe. "Where she'll have plenty of time to think about her crimes."

GLOSSARY

cargo hold area in a ship where objects are stored and carried

distract draw attention away from something

illusion something that appears to be real but isn't

Panama Canal narrow area of water that was dug across land in Panama to connect the Atlantic Ocean and Pacific Ocean

patrol protect and watch an area

port harbour where ships dock

precious having great value

quarters room or rooms on a ship where people live

sorceress woman who has magical powers

DISCUSS

1. Why does Circe use the mirror to create 12 versions of herself? What other ways could she have used her magic mirror against Wonder Woman?

2. Wonder Woman uses the power of her lasso to free herself from Circe's chains. What other powers or tools could she have used to break free?

3. Wonder Woman's lasso forces anyone it holds to tell the truth. Discuss a time in your life when a Lasso of Truth would have been helpful.

WRITE

1. If you had a magic mirror, what would it look like and what would it do? Write a short paragraph describing your mirror and draw a picture of it.

2. Imagine you one of the sailors Circe attacks with her magic snakes. Write about what it's like to get zapped to the ship's cargo hold.

3. At the end of the story, Wonder Woman says she is taking Circe to prison. Does she successfully deliver the villain there or does Circe escape along the way? Write a short story about what happens next.

AUTHOR

Michael Dahl is the author of more than 200 books for children and young adults, including *Bedtime for Batman*, *Be A Star, Wonder Woman!* and *Sweet Dreams, Supergirl*. He has won the AEP Distinguished Achievement Award three times for his non-fiction, a Teachers' Choice Award from *Learning* magazine and a Seal of Excellence from the Creative Child Awards. He is also the author of the Batman Tales of the Batcave and Superman Tales of the Fortress of Solitude series. Dahl currently lives in Minnesota, USA.

ILLUSTRATOR

Omar Lozano lives in Monterrey, Mexico. He has always been crazy about illustration and is constantly on the lookout for awesome things to draw. In his free time, he watches lots of films, reads fantasy and sci-fi books, and draws! Omar has worked for Marvel, DC, IDW, Capstone and several other publishers.